KT-372-192

This Edition first published 2002 by

MENTOR BOOKS
43 Furze Road,
Sandyford Industrial Estate,
Dublin 18.

Tel. (01) 295 2112/3   Fax. (01) 295 2114
e-mail: admin@mentorbooks.ie
www.mentorbooks.ie

ISBN: 1-84210-147-1

A catalogue record for this book is available from
the British Library

Text copyright © Cora Harrison 2002

The right of Cora Harrison to be identified as the Author
of the work has been asserted by her in accordance with the
Copyright Acts.

All rights reserved. No part of this publication may be
reproduced, stored in a retrieval system, or transmitted in any
form or by any means electronic, mechanical, photocopying,
recording, or otherwise, without prior written permission of the
publisher.

Illustrations: Ruth Ryan
Editing, Design and Layout by Mentor Books

Printed in Ireland by ColourBooks Ltd.

1 3 5 7 9 10 8 6 4 2

KA 1842 101471 9007

Dun Laoghaire-Rathdown Libraries
DEANSGRANGE LIBRARY
Inv/07 : L50J   Price E5.00
Title: General Field Mouse
Class: JF

General
Field Mouse

BAINTE DEN STOC

WITHDRAWN FROM
DÚN LAOGHAIRE-RATHDOWN COUNTY
LIBRARY STOCK

Written by

Cora Harrison

Illustrated by Ruth Ryan

Gráinseach an Déin
Deansgrange Library
Tel: 2850860

**MENTOR
BOOKS**

BAINTE DEN STOC

WITHDRAWN FROM DÚN LAOGHAIRE-RATHDOWN
COUNTY LIBRARY STOCK

To

Emma and
Brian Keyes

Once there was a little field mouse and his name was General Field Mouse.

General Field Mouse was very,
very brave.

He was the boss of all the field mice.

He lived in a little house by a big pond.

General Field Mouse liked his house. He liked to sit and to read by the fire when it was cold.

But when the sun was out, he liked to sit and to read beside the pond.

One day, General Field Mouse
was sitting by the pond when
he heard a lot of noise.

In the gate came lots of mice.
'The cats are coming,' they
squeaked.

There were big cats, small cats,
fat cats, thin cats.

There were black cats, white cats, striped cats, Siamese cats.

And every one of the cats had big, BIG eyes and sharp, SHARP, white teeth.

And every one of the cats was
HUNGRY!

Down the long roads, run, run, running came the cats.

Through the dark woods, creep,
creep, creeping came the cats.

Across the big fields, stalk, stalk, stalking came the cats.

'They'll be here soon,' said Tom
Mouse.

'I'll get Mr Dog to help us,' said
Mary Mouse.

'I can't help you,' said Mr Dog.
'I'm tied up just now.'

'I'll get Mr Fox to help us,' said
Mike Mouse.

'I can't help you,' said Mr Fox.
'Cats make me sneeze.'

'I'll get Mr Badger to help us,'
said Mr Baker-Mouse. 'He's very
brave.'

'Sorry,' said Mr Badger. 'I can't help you. I promised Mrs Badger I'd dig out another room for her new kitchen.'

'No one will help us,' said Mrs Baker-Mouse. 'The cats will eat us up.'

'We'll help ourselves,' said
General Field Mouse.

'What will we do?' asked Mary
Mouse.

'Listen to me, everyone,' said
General Field Mouse. 'I know
what we will do.'

Soon all the cats came to the garden gate.

And a big smile was on every cat's face.

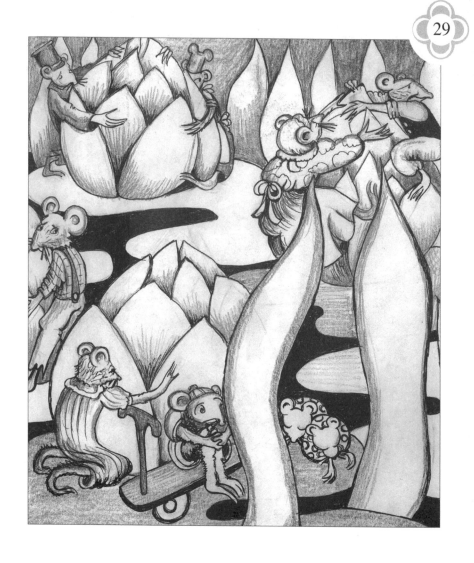

There in front of them were all
the field mice. And the field
mice looked very, very small.

And in front of all the field mice
was General Field Mouse.

And in his little paw was a SWORD.

And all the cats laughed and
laughed and laughed.

And, one by one, they began to
creep forward.

'I'll have the one with the little
toy sword,' said the cat with no
tail.

'I'll have the little girl one,' said the Siamese cat.

And the cats got nearer and
nearer to the edge of the pond.

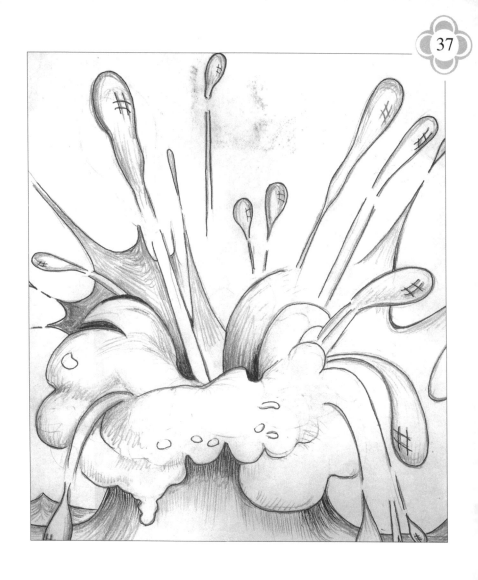

And SPLASH!

Every one of the cats fell through
the leaves and into the pond.

'I'll never look at a mouse again,' said one cat.

'Please help me, someone,' said another cat.

'I never did like water,' said a
big tom cat.

'Come back any time,' said
Mary Mouse.

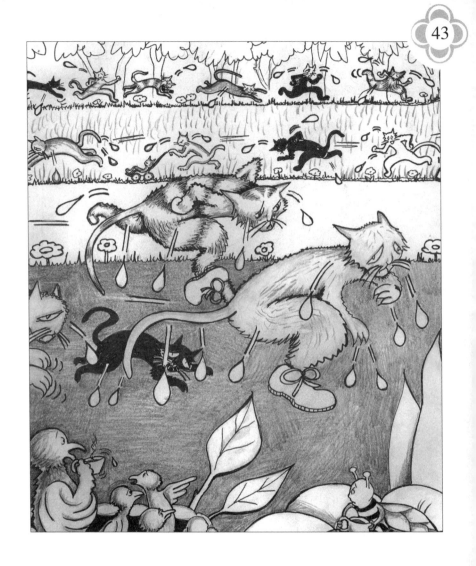

But those cats ran away down the road and they never came back again.

All the fieldmice had a big party.
And they all said 'Thank You' to
General Field Mouse.

Laabharlanna Dhún Laoghaire · Ráth An Dúin